MAGICAL MISPERCEPTION

SUZANNE G. ROGERS

IDUNN COURT PUBLISHING

Idunn Court Publishing
7 Ramshorn Court
Savannah, GA 31411
First published as *The Magical Misperception of Meridian* by MuseItUp Publishing, February 2012

Revised and expanded version published by Idunn Court Publishing, November 2014

✽ Created with Vellum

CONTENTS

THE QUEEN'S VISIT

*J*ona had a plan.

She crept downstairs, making sure to avoid the squeakiest treads. Her hand was on the doorknob when her mother pounced from out of nowhere and caught her by the suspenders.

"Jona Barbara Haever, you will not leave the house in those clothes! Queen Gaia will take you for a boy!"

"But I'm not actually meeting the queen," Jona protested. "And I want to have fun."

"You'll be sitting in the front row with your father and me, watching the presentation. Get that cap off your head and put on a dress, for heaven's sake. We're leaving soon."

"Yes, ma'am." The picture of contrition, Jona loped upstairs.

She had absolutely no intention of obeying her mother, of course. Her back-up plan involved a very serviceable drainpipe outside the window of her sister's room. When that room had been hers, she'd used it quite a few times to escape. Unfortunately, the neighbors had seen her climb down one night and told her parents. The aftermath had been unpleasant, and she'd been forced to switch rooms with Holly. At present, her challenge would be to reach the drainpipe before her sister sounded the alarm. If she were caught, the consequences would be swift and dire. Nevertheless, the benefits outweighed the risks on a day like today.

With an air of studied innocence, she sauntered into Holly's room. Her sixteen-year-old sister was a vision in a long, elegant lilac silk dress and brand-new kidskin slippers. Jona was impressed.

"What do you think?" Holly turned a slow pirouette. "Will I do?"

"You're the most beautiful girl in Ramshorn Village, but I don't know why you bought new shoes just for today. Queen Gaia isn't going to stare at your feet."

"Don't worry, these shoes are only for special occasions." Holly smiled. "They'll likely still be in good condition by the time you grow into them."

"I don't want the silly things," Jona said, quite truthfully. "They're far too fancy."

Holly perched herself in front of a vanity table and dusted her near perfect complexion with powder.

Jona stifled a sneeze. "I don't understand why the mayor picked you to give the queen a bouquet just because you're beautiful."

Holly pulled a hairbrush through her thick, glossy tresses. "When you begin to act a bit more ladylike, you'll get picked for things too. You're a pretty girl, Jona. Someday you'll want to show it."

Jona shook her head. "Why do people care so much what a girl looks like?"

"Why do you ask so many silly questions?" Holly shrugged. "They just do."

In contrast to her attractive, feminine sister, twelve-year-old Jona usually chose to wear boys' trousers, shirts, and suspenders. Although her thick blond hair was long and wavy, she always wore it in braids, tucked under a boy's cap—at least whenever possible. This manner of attire had started shortly after her elder sister had blossomed into a beauty.

While her sister fussed with different hairstyles, Jona edged toward the closed window. "It's awfully stuffy in here. Do you mind if I—"

"Ugh!" Holly threw down her hairbrush in exasperation. "My hair is impossible today!" She ran into the hallway and leaned over the staircase railing, clutching her tresses in both hands. "Mother, I need your help! I look dreadful!"

Jona couldn't believe her good fortune. Not about to spit in the eye of a golden opportunity, she unlatched the window and pushed it open. With athletic, practiced ease, she swung herself out onto the drainpipe and climbed down into the spring sunshine. When her feet hit the lawn, she sprinted for the hedge. One easy leap put her on the other side.

As Jona flew down the street, laughing with joy, she reveled in her freedom. She knew she'd have to answer for her disobedience eventually, but she'd worry about that later. Perhaps her mother would be so giddy after seeing the queen up close, she'd forget about any punishment for an errant daughter.

A block away from home, she slowed down to admire her surroundings. Ramshorn Village had been scrubbed, polished, and manicured for weeks in preparation for the queen's visit. Patriotic Meridian flags waved from each abode. Freshly planted perennials lent color to every flowerbed. Canopies, stages, grandstands, and food stalls had been erected downtown, and with a pocketful of coins saved for the occasion, Jona intended to thoroughly enjoy herself.

When she reached the town square, her nose led her to a booth selling hot, fragrant deep-fried doughnuts covered with powdered sugar. After buying a paper cone full of the treats, Jona climbed her favorite chestnut tree. From her perch overlooking the park, she had a good view of all the activity. Some of her friends had taken jobs for the day, selling festive pinwheels, tiny Meridian flags, or bags of candied fruit peels to the crowd. Several of the younger children had been enlisted to pick up after the horses. Because Jona had been expected to watch her sister meet the queen, she'd been exempted from service. Since she had no wish to encounter her mother, however, she remained out of sight in the tree.

In addition to the many familiar faces, she saw a huge number of strangers. Queen Gaia rarely ventured from her palace, so people had journeyed from miles around Ramshorn Village to see her. Many of Jona's neighbors had found themselves hosting near and distant relatives. Her parents' business, the Haever Tea Shop, had been sold out of tea for days and had had to resort to selling coffee.

As Jona finished her doughnuts, Her Majesty's entourage finally arrived. The school marching band played a patriotic, rousing tune, and Mayor Vanderbleat gathered on the stage with Holly and an array of prominent people. Even the local wizard, Canta, had been invited. The fellow wasn't much of a wizard, in Jona's opinion, but he could produce fireworks. He'd given a fairly decent show the previous evening after sundown.

When Queen Gaia was escorted onto the stage, the thunderous applause nearly shook Jona out of the tree. Holly sank into a graceful curtsy for the queen and presented her with an armful of carefully selected, thorn-free roses. Jona thought her sister did a splendid job, and her chest swelled with pride. After the speeches began, however, she quickly grew restive.

Glancing around for some real fun, her attention was drawn to a mostly empty street a short distance away. A boy about her age was jumping around and wielding a long stick. As he began practicing what looked like swordplay, she dropped to the lawn, found a stick of her own, and hastened toward him. She might have expected him to see her approach, but he seemed to be absorbed in a fight for his life.

"Stand fast, ye blighted highwaymen!" she overheard him exclaim. "Prepare to answer for your wickedness!"

The boy proceeded to engage said unseen bandits, running several of them through, repeatedly. Jumping into the fray, Jona began to fight alongside.

"I have your back, sir." She parried and thrust with her stick. "Two dozen against one is an unfair fight!"

"I welcome your assistance, stranger!" The boy's voice rang out. "These knaves are devilishly hard to kill."

Imaginary brigands surrounded the pair. Jona and her new friend fought the scurrilous villains with panache, in her opinion. An unlimited supply of pretend throwing knives was tucked into her waistband. Her aim was always true, and her blades were instantly lethal. As the fight unfolded, she discovered her partner had a fantastic, wily invisible bullwhip at his disposal. After a protracted, lengthy melee, the highwaymen were defeated at last.

The boy pumped Jona's hand in victory. "Thanks, friend. I thought I would certainly be overrun this time."

"Call me Jona."

"Lee." He mopped his brow with a shirtsleeve.

"You thirsty?"

He grimaced. "A bit, but I haven't any money."

"That's all right. I have some, and lemonade doesn't cost much anyway. Follow me."

Dropping their sticks, the two hastened toward the town square. Her Majesty had taken the stage, and as she droned on in a lengthy speech, Jona and Lee downed two big mugs of lemonade apiece.

She set her glass down on a nearby table. "Want to see the river?"

"Sure."

The two darted off together with Jona leading the way. At the broad, gentle Meridian River, they surveyed the boats moored to the dock. One of the local fishermen, Mr. Pikerman, wagged his finger at her. "Stay away from my fish traps, Jona Haever!"

"Yes, sir." She cleared her throat. "Why aren't you listening to Her Majesty's speech?"

He mopped his brow with a handkerchief. "There's work to be done, child."

Mr. Pikerman ambled past on his way to the end of the pier, and Jona rolled her eyes.

Lee lowered his voice. "What was that about?"

She sighed. "Two years ago, I opened Mr. Pikerman's traps and he still hasn't forgiven me."

"Why'd you do it?"

"I felt sorry for the fish."

Lee smothered a laugh.

Jona cast about for a topic of conversation. "So you're in town for the queen, I guess. Did you come with your parents?"

"Not with my parents, no. My aunt brought me. I don't have parents...they're dead."

Jona was taken aback. "That's really sad." She stared at her boots. "Er...I have a friend called Ned, whose mother got sick and died last year. It's been hard on him. It must be awful not to have parents."

He shrugged. "I never knew my parents. They died when I was a baby, I'm told."

"Um...do you like your aunt?"

He seemed to shrink into his clothes. "She's k-kind of scary, actually. I call her The D-Dragon."

Jona peered at him. "We don't have to talk about her if you don't want to." She pointed toward a pack of local kids flocking their way. "Oh look, some of my schoolmates are here. Maybe we can think up a good game."

As it so happened, her friend, Catrina, was among the group.

She eyed Lee with admiration and quickly pulled Jona to one side. "Introduce me to that gorgeous boy, will you?"

Jona glanced at Lee. They'd been having so much fun, she hadn't noticed he was handsome. Although his looks didn't make much difference to her one way or the other, she supposed Catrina was right.

She beckoned Lee over. "Lee, this is Catrina. She sits next to me in school."

Catrina curtsied and gave him her prettiest smile. "It's a pleasure."

To Jona's dismay, Lee's face flushed scarlet, almost as if he were having some kind of fit.

"N-N-Nice t-t-to m-m-meet you." He barely managed to force the words out.

When Jona's friends laughed, her hackles began to rise. Lee's obvious misery at their ridicule cut her to the core, and Catrina's giggles earned her a sharp elbow to the ribs.

"Stop it," Jona whispered.

Catrina composed herself, but the boys continued to mock Lee. The biggest one, Quinton, even pretended to choke himself.

"Cut it out, Quinton." Jona scowled. "It's not funny."

"S-S-Sorry, J-J-Jona," he chortled. "I c-c-can't s-s-stop m-m-myself."

Any feeling of friendship she'd ever felt toward Quinton rapidly dwindled. Her knuckles showed white as she balled her fists.

"I'm warning you to shut your mouth or I'll shut it for you."

"W-W-Whatever you s-s-say."

Without hesitation, Jona sank her fist into Quinton's stomach. As he bent double, the other boys piled on, and an all-out brawl ensued. The girls ran back to the celebration, screaming, while Jona and Lee fought off five boys together.

Finally, Mr. Pikerman came over and separated everyone.

"Fine behavior for the queen's visit." He made shooing motions with his gnarled hands. "Be off, the lot of ye."

Quinton and his friends stumbled away to nurse an assortment of black eyes, sore ribs, and scraped skin. Jona and Lee were left standing there, their chests heaving with exertion and indignation. Jona bent to retrieve her cap, which had been knocked to the ground in the scuffle and her waist-length braids tumbled over her shoulders like golden ropes. As Lee stared at her, his jaw dropped.

Jona gave him a puzzled glance. "What's wrong?"

"Well…you're a girl!"

Jona wiped a trickle of blood from her mouth with the back of her hand. "Yeah, so?"

"I can talk to you."

She narrowed her eyes. "Are you making fun of me?"

"No." Lee hunched his shoulders. "You might have noticed, I have trouble talking to girls."

Jona shrugged. "Maybe I did…a little."

"Come on." He beckoned. "I want you to meet my aunt."

"I don't know if I want to meet The Dragon." Jona made an exaggerated grimace.

He laughed at her expression. "It'll be all right. I'll protect you."

Her chin lifted. "Ha! Chances are good I'll have to protect you!"

They doubled back to the town square, where the speeches had concluded. Lee looked stricken. "Uh-oh, I'm late."

Jona almost lost sight of him as he darted into the throng of people, but she followed as best she could. Unfortunately, Lee was moving so quickly he smacked right into one of the queen's guards.

"Where are you going, you little troublemaker?" The guard grabbed Lee by the arm. "You're not supposed to be here!"

Jona jumped into action. "Hey, let go of him! He didn't do anything wrong!"

The guard ignored her and dragged Lee away as if he were a sack of potatoes.

"Lee!" Jona cried. "Run!"

Although the boy tried to squirm free, the queen's entourage was about to depart, and people were surging forward to catch a final glimpse. Jona and Lee were separated, and it was all she could do to avoid getting crushed. To her relief, her father swooped down and pulled her away from the danger. When they were clear of the crowd, however, the scolding began.

"Where have you been? You should have been sitting with us and we've been worried sick!"

Jona hung her head. "Sorry about that. I met a new friend and we went off to play near the river."

"You look a mess." A crease formed between Mr. Haever's eyebrows. "You haven't been fighting, have you?"

"Maybe a bit," she admitted. "I couldn't avoid it, though. The other kids were teasing Lee something awful and somebody had to stick up for him."

"I can't stand bullies." A proud grin played around her father's mouth. "Just between you and me, I hope you gave 'em what for."

His reaction surprised her, and she suddenly realized how fortunate she was to have such a wonderful father. She threw her arms around his waist and buried her face in his shirt.

"I love you," she mumbled.

Mr. Haever chuckled as he gave her a hug. "I love you too. What's this about?"

"Nothing...it's just that Lee doesn't have parents to take care of him, and I do. I'm really lucky."

"Let's get you cleaned up before your mother sees you, otherwise your luck won't hold."

At home, Jona washed the bloodstains off before her mother

saw her, and she explained her scrapes by pretending she'd fallen out of a tree. Nevertheless, her morning escape cost her a long lecture, several extra chores, and no dinner. Fortunately, Holly smuggled a sandwich to her room. For the second time that day, Jona was grateful for her family.

"Thank you. You know, I was really proud of you today." Jona snickered. "George Merkin couldn't keep his eyes off you."

Holly blushed. "Really?" A soft smile crept onto her rosebud lips. "I didn't think I'd ever get him to notice me."

Jona stared at her with consternation. "You like him back?"

"Of course!"

"I thought you hated him!"

"That was last year."

Holly left the room with a skip in her step. After the door closed, Jona rolled her eyes. "I'm never going to understand romance!"

As she chewed thinly sliced roast beef nestled between two soft pieces of rosemary bread, Jona wished she knew Lee's fate. That guard had looked quite angry, but he couldn't throw Lee in jail for bumping into him, could he? As she realized she would never see her new friend again, her sandwich suddenly didn't taste quite as good.

MERIDIAN PALACE

By the time the next school day came around, everyone except for Jona had largely forgotten the dockside scuffle. Although she didn't make a big point of it, she made sure to give Quinton a wide berth. Life was too short to hold a grudge and, like her classmates, she was counting the handful of days until the school year was over. While gazing out the window during math class, Jona daydreamed about all the swimming holes to be investigated, ripe plums and berries to be eaten, and shoes to be ignored. She planned to learn how to fish with a spear whittled from a hardwood sapling, and to improve her aim spitting watermelon seeds. Summer promised to be glorious.

On the final day of the term, a fancy carriage, flying the royal flag of Meridian, waited in front of the school. Rumors and speculation about an illustrious visitor ran rampant through the school halls, but nobody seemed to know anything. Just after the beginning bell rang, however, a note was delivered to Jona's teacher. He perused its contents before fixing Jona with his gaze.

"Miss Haever? You're wanted in the headmaster's office."

The blood left her face, and everyone turned to stare.

"What did you do?" Catrina whispered.

Beyond dismayed, Jona could only shake her head. Some of her friends gave her sympathetic smiles as she stood and walked down the aisle, but Quinton smirked and stuck his foot out to trip her. Jona smirked back and stomped on it.

"Oops, sorry."

His howl of pain was scant satisfaction as she trudged through the door and down the hall to meet her doom. She'd been called to Mr. Widgette's office only once before, when she'd accidentally-on-purpose poured ink down the front of Chet Bettle's trousers for calling Holly stuck-up. If she'd somehow managed to get expelled on the last day of school, her mother was not going to be pleased.

When she entered the headmaster's office, Mr. Widgette rose from behind his desk.

"Thank you for coming, Jona. A special guest has graced our school with his presence."

She noticed a strange little man sitting in a corner chair, dressed in an expensive suit.

"This is Mr. Phipps." The headmaster gestured toward the gentleman in the corner. "He is Her Majesty's representative."

Proper etiquette demanded she acknowledge the man in some fashion, so Jona gave him a wobbling curtsy. Then, feeling foolish, she wondered if she ought to have stuck out her hand instead.

Mr. Widgette cleared his throat. "Jona, Mr. Phipps would like to have a word with you."

In the silence that followed, she waited for someone to start laughing and let her in on the joke, but nobody did. Instead, the strange man leaned forward, fixing her with his oddly piercing gaze. "Miss Haever, the headmaster tells me your parents own a tea shop?"

She was bewildered. "Yes, that's right. They also sell coffee."

"Excellent." Mr. Phipps' smile was reassuring. "I'm sure their tea and coffee are splendid."

"Everyone says so." Jona shifted her weight. "People drive to Ramshorn Village from miles around, just to visit the shop."

"I can well imagine." He paused. "I expect you are wondering why I've come to speak with you today."

"Yes." Jona bit her lip. "I'm not in any trouble, am I?"

"Far from it." Mr. Phipps' manner turned businesslike. "Her Royal Majesty, Queen Gaia, would consider it a personal favor if you would live at the palace for the summer and assist her in a matter of some delicacy. In return, you would be paid a salary and your parents' tea shop would be awarded a Royal Warrant."

A relieved grin spread across Jona's features. "That's very generous, sir, but I think you must be looking for my sister, Holly. I'll go fetch her if you'd like."

"No, Her Majesty is most definitely looking for *you*, Miss Jona Haever," Mr. Phipps said. "Mr. Widgette has agreed to release you from school this morning. If you would be so kind as to accompany me in my carriage, we'll drive to the Haever Tea Shop and discuss the matter with your parents."

Her eyes swiveled toward the headmaster, who nodded. "Go gather your things, Jona. It seems your summer vacation begins a little early this year."

When the royal carriage rolled up to the tea shop, Jona watched her parents come to the window, to stare. Their expressions turned to shock when their youngest daughter leaped onto the pavement, followed by a strange, well-dressed little man. Mr. Phipps explained the opportunity to them, and they were as bewildered as Jona had been at this odd turn of events.

"Merciful heavens." Her mother untied her shop apron. "I must go home and pack Jona's trunk!"

"There's no need, Mrs. Haever," Mr. Phipps replied. "Everything your daughter could possibly require will be provided for her, I can assure you."

Her parents hugged and kissed her good-bye. Then, still clad in her school uniform pinafore dress, she was bundled back into the carriage. As the horses began to move, she couldn't stifle a giggle. Mr. Phipps gave her an inquiring glance.

"I'm on my way to the palace." Jona beamed. "My friend Catrina will be so envious."

He gave her a placid smile. As the journey began, Jona wasn't quite sure what to do with herself. After a few minutes admiring the luxurious upholstery of the carriage and the speed at which they were moving, however, the novelty wore thin. Mr. Phipps sat quietly with his manicured hands resting gently on top of his jeweled-head walking stick. Neither young nor old, he stared straight ahead with a composed, oddly regal expression that Jona quite admired, considering she couldn't stop fidgeting.

"How long before we reach the palace?" she blurted out.

"Several hours."

"What are my duties likely to be?"

"That is for you and Her Majesty to discuss."

At that point, Mr. Phipps shut his eyes, signaling the end of the conversation. With a sigh, Jona focused on the passing terrain. They'd left Ramshorn Village behind and were now in the countryside. Having never traveled this far from town before, she gawked at the neat and tidy vineyards, orchards, and flocks of farm animals. After a while, though, even the scenery became tedious.

Her thoughts turned to school. Sadly, she'd missed her classroom party and the end-of-term assembly. She'd been due to receive a ribbon for running the fastest footrace at Field Day, although her sister would certainly bring it home for her. When she remembered she hadn't said good-bye to Holly, a pang of regret made her bite her lower lip. As the pangs continued, she realized she was also quite hungry. Her stomach began to growl in a loud and insistent fashion. Embarrassed, she folded her arms across her waist, hoping to muffle the noise, but her efforts were useless.

Eventually, Mr. Phipps opened his eyes and signaled the driver to stop at the next inn. Once there, Jona satisfied her hunger with an enormous chicken pie and as much sweet lemonade as she could drink. She was glad for the respite because the next leg of their journey took at least as long as the first half. Although she dozed through a large part of it, when they reached the outskirts of Meridian City, she was awakened by noise from all the traffic and commerce.

Jona practically hung out the window in awe, gaping at the shiny open-air rigs filled with well-dressed people in fancy hats. Much stronger magic was at work here than could be found in Ramshorn Village, she noticed. To her delight, some of the shop signs were inexplicably glowing with light or rotating slowly, and a few of the more ornate carriages had been enchanted to move without horses.

Jona caught Mr. Phipps' eye. "Why doesn't this carriage move without horses?"

"It does. The team of horses out front is actually an illusion created by the Wizard Farland. Her Majesty likes the appearance of horse-drawn carriages, but without the mess."

Jona gasped at the mention of the Wizard Farland. Next to the queen, the wizard was the most famous person in Meridian. She could scarcely dare hope to meet him; none of her friends would believe it if she did.

"Does the Wizard Farland live at the palace?" she ventured.

"Although he is a frequent visitor, the good wizard has a home of his own."

The carriage drove through the center of town, where the buildings were four and five stories high. Jona wondered how the structures didn't just fall over, but she supposed they were under enchantments as well. They passed a park with a fountain spewing not water, but colored sparks, much like one of Canta's fireworks shows. At that same park, mothers fondly supervised young children as they bounced up and down on a section of emerald grass magically rendered springy. It looked like so much fun, Jona wished she could have a go herself.

Eventually, Meridian Palace came into view—larger than any man-made structure she'd ever seen. Situated on a hill, the palace was constructed of glistening ivory stones with a pearly gleam. After guards waved them through an imposing arched gateway, the carriage drove up a meandering drive. The road was completely covered by a canopy of oak tree branches festooned with lacy, hanging moss. Movement beyond the oaks revealed the existence of dainty, white-tailed deer, colorful, preening peacocks, and playful black squirrels. The palace grounds were quite extensive, and it was actually several miles from the gate until they reached the courtyard.

At long last, the carriage rolled to a stop, and Mr. Phipps climbed out. "Good luck, Miss Haever. Wait here, if you please." As he spoke, he had a kindly twinkle in his eye. "We'll be seeing each other again quite soon."

Jona remained in her seat. "Thank you."

After he strode off, her mouth suddenly went dry and her hands became icy. She'd never been out of Ramshorn Village before, and here she was at Meridian Palace, surrounded by splendor. What could she possibly have to offer anyone in such a place?

Moments later, a matron appeared in the doorway and motioned Jona to step down from the carriage. "Come, child, let's not dawdle."

Jona wasn't one to be intimidated easily, but when she

emerged from the carriage and into the impressive courtyard, she felt tiny and insignificant. Confronted with magnificent architecture, manicured bushes, and glorious statuary, she wasn't sure where to glance first.

The matron cured that problem right away. "My name is Nanny Phipps." Her manner was no-nonsense. "I'll be tending to your needs."

"Yes, ma'am." Jona frowned. "Are you related to Mr. Phipps, by any chance?"

"He is my husband."

Jona followed her up marble staircases, through wide, carpeted hallways, and past so many doorways, she knew she'd never be able to find her way back to the courtyard without help. Nanny moved quickly for such a stout woman. When they finally reached Jona's bedroom, Nanny handed her a dress, white stockings, and slippers.

"Change into these, dear."

Jona's eyes widened in admiration. "How pretty!"

Whereas her school uniform was starchy gray and white cotton, this new dress was a sumptuous sky-blue silk with snowy lace trim. Her leather boots were a trifle worse for wear, but her new blue slippers were lighter and even more beautifully made than the ones Holly had purchased for her big moment with the queen.

As Jona slid her feet into the shoes, they fit her feet as if they'd been made to measure. "How did you know my size?"

"Magic, of course. The Wizard Farland has many clever enchantments up his sleeves."

A shiver of excitement ran down Jona's spine at the thought of wearing clothes and shoes enchanted by the most revered wizard in the kingdom. "I expect so."

Once Jona was dressed, Nanny quickly loosened her braids and brushed out her hair until it shone.

"You have lovely hair, child."

"It's nothing when compared to my sister, Holly. She's the prettiest girl in Ramshorn Village."

"I expect when you are older, you will give her a run for her money."

"You've never seen Holly. In fact, she should be here instead of me." Jona met the woman's gaze in the vanity mirror. "I don't even know why I've been summoned."

"Her Majesty must have her reasons."

Nanny arranged Jona's tresses into a ponytail at the base of her neck and tied on a fat bow. Although she wouldn't dream of saying so, Jona felt rather like a pampered poodle.

As Nanny worked, she gave Jona instructions. "When you meet Her Majesty, you're not to speak unless you are spoken to. An audience with the queen is a privilege and an honor accorded to few, and you're expected to act appropriately."

"Yes, ma'am."

The matron made a tsking sound with her tongue. "Your hair is far too wild and your fingernails are a scandal, but it can't be helped at the moment. I've been told you're to be brought around as soon as you arrive. We'll fix the rest later." She stepped back. "Let's go."

The formidable woman strode from the room with Jona scampering to keep up. They wound their way once more through the labyrinth-like palace until they arrived at the open doorway of a large solarium filled with plants.

Suddenly seized by nerves, Jona hung back. "Is the queen really in there?"

"Yes, but she won't bite you, lass." Nanny winked and patted her on the shoulder. "Go on. You've a friend waiting for you, too."

A friend? Consumed with curiosity, Jona edged through a jungle of exotic ferns and potted palms until she reached a sitting area. When she saw Lee standing there, a rush of pleasure made her nearly cry out. She hastened toward him, but he gave her a little frown and a shake of his head. Momentarily confused, she paused long enough to notice Queen Gaia in the corner, pruning a bonsai tree. Jona's jaw dropped, and she bit back a gasp.

Lee cleared his throat to get the queen's attention. "Your M-Majesty? Miss H-Haever has arrived."

The queen glanced up. "So she has." Putting down her shears, the woman studied Jona for a moment. "I understand you are acquainted with my nephew?"

Unable to speak, Jona nodded.

"Lee is in need of socialization and has requested your presence over the summer holiday to assist him. You'll provide him with a partner as he learns to dance and make polite conversation. I daresay you're in need of a little socialization yourself."

Wondering if she should speak, Jona flicked a glance at Lee. He gave her an encouraging nod.

"Yes, Your Majesty." She curtsied, for good measure.

"Tonight you will both dine with the royal tutor, Mr. Phipps, and his wife. You'll learn manners, proper etiquette, and the art of discourse. Tomorrow, you'll receive dancing instruction from Mr. Rapp." Queen Gaia flicked her fingertips in a shooing motion. "Both of you may go."

Lee bowed to his aunt, and Jona sketched a curtsy again. They left the solarium together at a sedate walk, but as soon as the door closed, Jona gave Lee a good-natured push.

"I've been worried about you!" she cried. "Why didn't you tell me who you were?"

He made a face. "Why didn't you tell me you were a girl?"

"I didn't think it was important."

"Same."

After a moment, they burst into giggles.

Lee edged down the hall. "You want to see my favorite room in the palace?"

"Definitely."

Lee ushered Jona into the library, where handsome leather-bound volumes lined the shelves from floor to ceiling. Jona ran her fingertips along the bindings, which were embossed in gold. After they took turns riding on the sliding ladder, they clambered up onto a wide window seat framed by velvet drapes. Flat, embroidered cushions and a myriad of throw pillows rendered the cozy space comfortable.

"If you pull these curtains together, this is a great place to hide." Lee demonstrated. "In winter, I read in here for hours."

"What sort of books do you read?"

"Adventure books, naturally. What other kinds are there?"

Jona admired the view through the leaded-glass windows. Opulent gardens stretched before her, verdant and dazzling in the afternoon sunshine.

She pressed her nose as close as possible to the window pane without touching it. "I've never seen anything so gorgeous. Are we allowed outside?"

"Of course." Lee jumped off the window seat and pulled back the curtains. "Come on."

With Jona hot on his heels, he darted from the library and raced through the carpeted hallways. When they reached the garden, they played a game of tag on the white gravel paths crisscrossing the exquisite rose beds.

Jona spied a picturesque bridge nearby spanning a narrow, meandering lagoon. "What's over that way?" She pointed.

"The fruit and vegetable gardens." His expression turned mischievous. "You want to steal some blackberries?"

"Won't we get in trouble?"

Lee gave her a sidelong glance. "What are they going to do, kick me out?"

"You have a point."

This time, Jona led the way across the wooden bridge and through an arched opening made of fragrant, flowering vines. Lee chased her through a manicured field of grass so fine, the texture resembled the velvet curtains in the library. Long before Jona saw the vegetable garden, she could smell its rich, pungent soil. Tidy, fenced-in rows of green beans, corn, tomatoes, lettuce, squash, and carrots stretched out in a colorful array, hemmed in by a painted white fence designed to keep the deer at bay.

"Your gardens are so well-tended." She tweaked the fern-like top of a carrot. "I bet rabbits wouldn't dare trespass!"

Lee waved a dismissive hand. "This is the boring stuff. The fruit orchards are much more interesting."

After they passed groves of peach and cherry trees, the two friends finally wound up at the blackberry bushes. Lee picked a massive number of berries and squished them into his mouth. "Mmm!" Dark juice dribbled down his chin when he smiled. "Have some."

"If you're sure." Jona pulled sun-ripened berries from the bush until her hand overflowed. As she bit down on the fruit, sweet tangy flavor exploded on her tongue. "Delicious!"

They concentrated on eating berries for several minutes until they could hold no more. Then, with a mischievous giggle, Jona picked a handful and lobbed them at Lee. The berries made purplish splotches on his starched white shirt, and several found their way down his collar.

"Hey! Why'd you do that?"

She feigned pique. "That's for not telling me your aunt was the queen."

"Oh yeah? This means war!"

As Lee snatched berries off the bush with intensity built on revenge, Jona fled through the orchard, shrieking with laughter. Lee sprinted after her, throwing berry after berry. She fought back with little green peaches until one of her missiles hit Lee on the head.

"Ow!" Lee protested. "No fair."

"Sorry!"

Realizing she needed juicier ammunition, she ducked into the cherry orchard. Just as she was about to hurl a cluster of ripe fruit, a booming voice rang out. "What do you think you're doing, you little hooligan?"

A huge hand descended on Jona's shoulder, pinning her in place. Panic-stricken, she accidentally squished the cherries in her fist. Red juice dripped from her trembling fingers onto her captor's shoes.

He scowled. "Why, I ought to—"

Lee rushed over, radiating shame and regret. "I'm s-sorry, Mr. McKinney, this is entirely my fault. I wanted to play 'war,' and I guess we got a little c-c-carried away. I'm ever so sorry."

Following Lee's lead, Jona hung her head in contrition. "Forgive me, sir. I didn't mean any harm."

"Mr. McKinney?" Lee peeked at the groundskeeper through the lock of hair that fell down onto his forehead. "Hanna asked about you the other day."

The man's outrage seemed to ebb a trifle. "She did, did she?"

"Yeah. I told her there was no groundskeeper as talented as our Mr. McKinney."

After a long pause, the tall, dour man roared with laughter. "You're full of beans, Your Highness. All right, you and your friend go on...but don't let me catch you destroying my orchards again."

Lee shook his head. "No, sir. We won't."

Mr. McKinney gave him an appraising glance. "Wait a minute." He reached into a nearby cart and lifted out a pint basket of ripe cherries. "Give that to Hanna—with my compliments."

"I will, sir." Lee jerked his head at Jona. "We should be going."

They hastened off, but when Jona glanced back, Mr. McKinney was still chuckling.

"Who's Hanna?" Jona whispered.

"She's one of the upstairs maids. Mr. McKinney's sweet on her."

Jona blinked. "Does she like him as well?"

He waggled his eyebrows. "She will after I give her these cherries."

Jona gave Lee an admiring smile. "You handled Mr. McKinney beautifully. Thanks for getting me out of trouble, by the way. It was very gallant of you to come to my rescue."

Lee waved off her thanks. "You're not in the clear. Just wait until Nanny Phipps sees your dress."

Jona glanced down at the stained frock and groaned. "I'm doomed."

WIZARD FARLAND

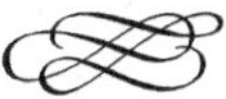

As the days at Meridian Palace unfolded, Jona treasured each one. Her favorite part was spending time with Lee outside of lessons, when they invented games in the gardens. Sometimes they were heroes and sometimes villains, but they were almost always on the same side.

The lessons themselves weren't bad, either. Although her mother had taught her regular manners, Jona would never again have to wonder which fork or spoon to use for what purpose. Learning how to dance with Lee, however, made her feel self-conscious and awkward. She suspected he felt the same way, because he couldn't keep a straight face. At their first lesson, they kept dissolving into laughter, leaving Mr. Rapp peevish and cross. After an hour of working with them in the ballroom, the dance instructor threw up his hands in disgust.

"It appears I'm wasting my time," he snapped. "If you two cannot take this more seriously tomorrow, I'll be forced to inform Her Majesty."

He stormed out, followed by his mousy pianist. Jona and Lee suddenly became somber.

"Oh, no." She gave Lee a worried glance. "If Mr. Rapp tells

The Dragon we aren't learning to dance properly, I'll probably be sent home in disgrace."

A crease formed on Lee's forehead. "I don't want you to go. We'll just have to impress Mr. Rapp."

"How?"

"We'll find a way." His nod was decisive.

That night, after everyone had retired, they sneaked into the ballroom to practice. Lee turned up one of the gas lamps just enough that they wouldn't trip in the dark. As they faced one another next to the piano, Jona could still feel the awkwardness between them.

She took a deep breath and let it out. "Um…maybe it would help if we make a game of it."

"Like what?"

"Well, we'll be different people. You can be a handsome prince—"

"Naturally." He sketched a courtly bow. "At least you've got the prince part right."

Jona giggled. "And I'll be a beautiful damsel who's under an enchantment. Mr. Rapp is an evil sorcerer, you know."

"Evil, you say? I knew it all along." Lee lifted an eyebrow. "What wicked enchantment are you under?"

"From midnight until dawn, I turn into one of those peach trees in the garden."

He recoiled. "The black-hearted villain!"

"Yes, my arms get awfully tired by the time the sun comes up." She gave him a pained glance. "Each time we perfect a dance, however, it weakens Mr. Rapp's dastardly spell."

"I'm all about rescuing damsels and weakening spells." Lee held out his arms. "Let's get to it."

She frowned. "It would be easier if we had music."

"Oh, but we do. The Wizard Farland enchanted this piano to play anything we want." Lee patted the instrument. "A waltz, if you please—but as quietly as you can."

"Good idea." Jona nodded. "We don't want to alert Mr. Rapp's minions."

When the instrument responded with a barely-audible tune played in three-quarter time, Jona clapped her hands in delight. "How perfect. I do so love magic!"

Cloaked in the guise of a game, Jona and Lee discovered learning to dance was much easier—especially when the lighting was dim. After an hour of hard practice, they could waltz together in a creditable fashion.

"I can hardly wait to see Mr. Rapp's face when he sees us dance tomorrow," Lee said. "He'll probably think it's because he's a brilliant teacher."

Jona stifled a yawn. "As long as he doesn't report me to your aunt, I don't care if he considers himself the best teacher in Meridian."

THE NEXT MORNING, Jona and Lee arrived for their dance lesson with dark circles under their eyes.

Mr. Rapp peered at them with ill-concealed disdain. "I can see we won't be making much progress again."

"Sorry, Mr. Rapp. I couldn't sleep last night." Jona gave the instructor a sweet smile. "I felt so bad about disappointing you yesterday."

"I had trouble sleeping, too." Lee shook his head. "Whenever I fell asleep, however, I dreamed about the waltz."

Jona and Lee exchanged an amused glance, which didn't escape the dance teacher's notice. His sigh held a note of resignation. "Yes, well, let's see if you retained anything from yesterday."

After Mr. Rapp nodded at the pianist, she began to play the opening notes to a waltz. With as much dignity as a handsome prince could muster, Lee led the enchanted damsel to the dance floor. The instructor seemed dumbstruck when his pupils began to waltz around the ballroom without hesitation. Even in the full light flooding the windows, Jona felt far less self-conscious than the day before.

"The sorcerer is not saying anything," she whispered.

Lee's gaze flickered toward Mr. Rapp. "We must have weakened his spell."

"Definitely." Jona grinned.

After that, their dance lessons were never quite as awkward. In addition, Mr. Phipps was happy to include Jona in Lee's regular lessons in archery, horsemanship, and fencing. She was not as accomplished at those activities as was Lee, but he, in turn, could never beat her when they raced back to the palace afterward. Lee's stutter became smoother and smoother as the weeks flew by, usually reappearing only when he was under stress.

To Jona's relief she had no occasion to see Queen Gaia—until the afternoon she and Lee were called to take tea with Her Majesty in the solarium. Nanny helped Jona dress beforehand, brushing her tresses more carefully than usual.

"I used to have beautiful hair, like yours," the woman reminisced.

As Jona stole a glance at the matron's thin, graying wisps, she couldn't imagine Nanny with a full mane.

"I always wanted a daughter," the older woman continued. "My son is very handsome, but I would have liked to have a daughter as well."

"Where is your son, Nanny?"

The woman flinched, nearly dropping the hairbrush to the floor. "Oh—he, um, d-died at fourteen months old."

"I'm so sorry." Jona stared at her, aghast.

"It was a long time ago. Lee reminds me of him so much that I sometimes think of him as my own." She tied a ribbon in Jona's hair. "There. You're a perfect lady."

"Thank you." Jona gave the woman an impulsive hug.

"No, thank *you*, child." Nanny patted Jona's cheek. "Mr. Phipps and I have never seen Lee this happy."

AT TEA, Jona made sure to cross her ankles and in all other ways comport herself properly. When the teacart came around, she took only two little sandwiches—even though they were her absolute favorite deviled ham—and she was careful to eat only one éclair. Every time she glanced at Lee, however, he gave her an impish grin gushing with creamy pastry filling. Jona stuck out her tongue in return whenever Queen Gaia's attention was engaged elsewhere.

"Lee, Mr. Rapp informs me you have applied yourself to your dancing lessons quite well," the queen said.

His face instantly assumed an innocent expression, and he was forced to swallow the pasty filling all at once. "Yes, I believe I have."

The woman stirred a teaspoon of sugar into her tea. "And I have heard from Mr. Phipps that your conversational skills are much improved."

"I think they are, Your Majesty."

"Good. I'll expect you to demonstrate your progress at our annual end-of-summer ball. The Wizard Farland has consented to provide the entertainment again."

Jona's excitement overflowed. "The Wizard Farland! How absolutely marvelous. I can hardly wait to meet him."

The queen peered at her in disapproval.

Jona bit her lip as she realized she'd spoken out of turn. "Er...forgive me."

"Miss Haever, your attendance at the ball would be entirely inappropriate," Queen Gaia said. "The household help do have a festive dinner of their own, to celebrate the occasion. You will be most welcome at that."

Jona gulped. "Thank you, Your Majesty."

She lowered her gaze to her plate. Despite the fact her cheeks were burning with humiliation, she tried to remain composed for Lee's sake. Her close friendship with him had caused her to forget her status, but Queen Gaia had just made it abundantly clear Jona Barbara Haever was a commoner—and a servant.

After their tea with the queen, Jona and Lee climbed the chestnut tree next to the veranda. The late afternoon sun sliced through the leaves, illuminating their branch with dappled light.

Lee railed against his aunt at length. "She's a mean old dragon. If y-you don't go to the ball, I don't want to go." He swelled with resentment. "It won't be any fun at all."

Jona managed a smile. "She's just observing protocol, Lee. As a member of the royal family, you have duties and responsibilities."

"I'll make a fool of myself without you. The Dragon will expect me to talk and dance with girls, and I'll begin stuttering again."

The image of Lee socializing with other girls caused a weird sort of twisting sensation in Jona's chest, but she pushed it aside.

"No, you won't. Every time you talk to a girl, just imagine you're talking to me. Better yet, picture her wearing trousers."

"That might work." Lee laughed. "You know what? You're my best friend."

The strange, twisting sensation ebbed, and Jona was filled with happiness. "Same."

～

THE NIGHT OF THE BALL, Lee stopped by Jona's room to show off his dashing formal suit with tails. Although he was somewhat ill at ease, he looked every bit the handsome young prince.

She clapped her hands in glee. "You're dazzling. Absolutely splendid! I'm really proud of you, and I know your aunt will be too."

Despite her praise, Lee's mouth turned down at the corners. "I sure wish you were going to be there."

"I have an idea." Jona pulled the red silk grosgrain hair ribbon from the end of her braid and handed it to him. "Tuck that in your pocket, and a part of me will be with you the whole time."

As Lee took the ribbon, a slight flush stained his cheeks. He folded the ribbon carefully, slid it into his pocket, and gave her a shy smile. Before she could think too hard about it, Jona deposited a kiss on his cheek. "You're going to do well."

His blushed deepened, and she wished she could guess his thoughts. Had she been too forward or crossed some sort of line?

Lee averted his eyes for a moment. "Thanks." He quickly kissed Jona's cheek before fleeing out the door.

Her initial rush of pleasure at Lee's gesture of affection gave way to despair. Her new trunk, a gift from Queen Gaia, was already packed for her departure, so she had little to distract her from her disappointment about the ball—or parting from Lee forever the next morning. He really was the best friend she'd ever had, and she felt even closer to him at that moment than anyone—including Catrina or her sister. She sank onto her bed and tried unsuccessfully to hold back tears. Even now she missed Lee, and they hadn't even said good-bye yet.

Jona had been invited to attend the household staff's end-of-summer banquet. Although she wasn't terribly hungry, she dried her tears and went down to the Servant's Hall anyway.

The specially prepared dishes looked and smelled wonderful, but she ended up pushing her food around on her plate. Not even a dessert of moist chocolate cake with cherry filling could rally her spirits. As lively conversation ebbed and flowed around the table, Jona stayed silent. Nanny and Mr. Phipps, who were sitting at the table directly across from her, tried to engage her in conversation, but could only elicit one word responses.

"Are you feeling well, child?" Nanny asked finally.

"Yes, thank you. It's just that," Jona swallowed the lump in her throat, "tonight's my last night here. I'm quite sad to go home."

Nanny and Mr. Phipps exchanged a glance.

"We'll all be sorry to lose you," Mr. Phipps said. "Lee, most especially."

At that, Jona could no longer suppress her emotions. With tears stinging her eyelids, she rose from the table. "If you'll excuse me, I should finish packing." Even to her own ears, her voice had a strangled quality. "Thank you for dinner."

The strains of music reached her ears as she left the Servant's Hall. Instead of climbing the stairs to the upper floor, she reversed course and tiptoed outside to the veranda. If she positioned herself right, she might be able to glimpse Lee dancing with a girl.

Jona shimmied up the chestnut tree, where she had an unobstructed view of the party. The ballroom was sparkling with light and filled with beautifully dressed couples. After a long while, she finally spotted Lee waltzing with a dainty blonde in a gorgeous lavender satin dress. Jona's heart melted and a proud smile crept onto her lips as she watched him dance. When Lee laughed at something the girl said, Jona laughed at the same time. If he was having any trouble talking to his partner, it wasn't at all obvious.

When the dance came to an end, an elegantly dressed, elderly man opened the glass-paneled doors wide and stepped outside. Jona froze as he walked onto the veranda and stood directly underneath her branch. She held her breath, hoping he wouldn't look up—to no avail. To her consternation, his bright blue eyes stared directly at her.

"Well, hello!" The gentleman gave her a beaming smile. "That can't possibly be comfortable. Would you like to join me? The view is much better down here, and we might be able to find you a small glass of champagne."

Jona found her tongue. "Thank you, but I haven't been invited."

"Perhaps not, but *I* have been, and I'd love for you to be my guest. My invitation was for two, but alas I came alone."

Jona jumped down from her perch and brushed bits of bark from her dress. She had no intention of being his guest, but neither did she wish to hold a conversation while sitting in a tree.

The fellow cocked his head. "That's better, isn't it?"

"Yes." She curtsied. "You're very kind, sir, but I must go before anyone sees me."

He glanced at the ballroom. "It's a miserable situation, being on the outside looking in, isn't it?"

"A little," she admitted.

He nodded. "I've often been the outsider myself. Please stay for one dance."

Jona edged back. "I'm sorry, but I'm not dressed properly."

A moment later, she found her everyday frock had been transformed into a stunning shell-pink satin gown. Her hair was now perfectly coiffed in a cascade of corkscrew curls, and she was even wearing an exquisite seed pearl necklace.

She gasped with pleasure. "It's beautiful!"

"I hope you like the color." He gestured toward her curls. "I saw your hair, and I thought pink. We can change it, if you prefer."

"It's absolutely perfect." Jona paused. "You must be the Wizard Farland."

"Must I? Yes, I suppose I must. And you?"

She was overcome by uncharacteristic shyness. "Jona Haever."

As the orchestra began to play the next song, music drifted out to the veranda. Farland bowed deeply. "May I have this dance, Miss Jona Haever?"

She sketched her most graceful curtsy. "I would be honored, kind sir."

They waltzed together on the veranda, and Jona was very glad for the excellent instruction Mr. Rapp had given her.

"You dance exceedingly well," Farland observed. "It's obvious you're not a servant."

"I am, if you ask Her Majesty." Jona bit her lip. "I'm actually a friend of Lee's. We shared lessons this summer."

The wizard frowned. "You're a friend of the prince and yet you're not invited to the ball? Seems a harsh business, to my way of thinking."

"No." She could not repress a sigh. "I'm not nobility or gentry."

Farland chuckled. "Neither am I."

"But you're unique."

"So are you." His eyes met hers. "I daresay you're one of a kind."

"There's a world of difference between me and the people in that ballroom."

"There doesn't have to be." He shrugged. "It's really all a matter of perception—or misperception, as the case may be."

Misperception? Before Jona could ask what he meant, the music ended and someone inside the ballroom announced the Wizard Farland.

He stepped back. "It seems I'm wanted. Thank you for the dance, Miss Jona Barbara Haever."

With that, he returned to the ballroom. The doors magically closed behind him, and Jona's magical finery faded away—from a butterfly back into a moth.

As she left the veranda and returned to her bedroom, she puzzled over her strange, unusual encounter with the most famous wizard in recent history.

How had the Wizard Farland known her middle name?

AFTER BREAKFAST THE NEXT MORNING, a royal carriage was brought around to the courtyard. While Nanny, Lee, and Jona said their good-byes, Jona's trunk was loaded into the boot.

Jona gave Nanny a big, warm hug. "Thank you for everything. I'll miss you terribly."

"And I'll miss you too, lass." The stout woman had a sudden case of the sniffles and had to blot her eyes with her apron.

Jona turned to Lee. "Thank you for bringing me here. This was the best summer I've ever had. I'll never forget it—or you."

"Same." He pressed a hinged wooden box into her hands. "This is one of a set that the Wizard Farland gave me last night. A message, put into one, will be transported to the other, by magic."

"Really?" Jona gaped at the carved box in amazement. "I've never owned anything magical before."

Lee's expression turned vulnerable. "Will you write to me? If you do, I promise to answer."

"Of course, I will." Jona hesitated, and then threw her arms around him. "I feel like I'm never going to see you again, Lee." Tears began to well up in her eyes.

His arms tightened around her. "I won't let that happen. You're my best friend, remember?"

Jona nodded. "Same."

When she stepped away from Lee, moisture was rimming

his eyes, too. As she climbed into the carriage, where Mr. Phipps was waiting to accompany her home, tears were streaming down Jona's face in earnest. The tutor pretended not to notice—until he was obliged to lend her his handkerchief.

THE INVITATION

Nine years later...

Jona filled a paper bag with two scoops of loose-leaf tea and folded the top over. "Here you are, Mr. Vanderbleat." She gave the bag to a handsome young man waiting on the far side of the counter.

He caught her wrist. "Oh, do call me Wallace."

Although she smiled to soften the blow, she freed herself from his grip. "That would be entirely inappropriate."

His eyebrows drew together. "Oh come now, Jona, we've known each other since you were in pigtails."

Her smile remained fixed. "Is there anything else you'd like?"

Mr. Vanderbleat sighed with resignation. "A dozen of those chocolate-dipped biscuits should do it. Mother enjoys them with her tea."

Jona's elder sister, who was sitting on a stool near the cash register, stood. "I'll get the biscuits."

While Holly filled a small pink box with the baked goods, Mr. Vanderbleat smirked at Jona with a cocksure grin. "Come out with me tomorrow night, and I'll take you to the best restaurant in town."

"You're kind, but with my parents away on holiday for the next few weeks, I must tend the shop."

He averted his gaze. "It seems like you're always working."

Jona's sister taped the box closed with a royal seal set on foil and lowered it to the counter. "A baker's dozen. We'll add it to your father's account."

"Thank you, Mrs. Merkin." As he picked up the box, Mr. Vanderbleat gave Jona a wink. "I'm not going to give up until you go out with me."

She ignored his words. "Have a good evening."

The young man left the shop with his tea and biscuits and strode out into the twilight, leaving Jona and her sister alone.

Holly confronted Jona with her arms akimbo. "Why didn't you agree to have dinner with him? You know perfectly well that I could have covered the shop tomorrow night by myself."

Fortunately for Jona, she was spared from having to answer when a man and a little boy entered the shop.

"Hullo!" George Merkin lifted his hand in a wave. "Boyd and I have come to walk his mummy home."

"Hullo, George!" Jona came out from behind the counter and knelt so the little boy could give her a hug. "How is my favorite nephew?"

As Jona cooed to the toddler, Holly and her husband exchanged a kiss.

"What's that in your ear?" Jona stood, peering at Boyd in mock surprise.

The tow-haired lad stared at her in wide-eyed confusion.

"I think it's a gingersnap!"

After Jona appeared to produce a biscuit from Boyd's ear, peals of childish laughter filled the shop. She gave him the treat so he could eat it.

George gave her an appreciative nod. "That was a neat trick."

"I learned my magic from the Wizard Farland himself, but I can teach it to you." Jona winked and showed George how she'd palmed the biscuit.

Her brother-in-law snickered. "I'll have to try that with vegetables. Maybe Boyd will like them better then."

"Somehow, I don't think it works that way." Jona turned to her sister. "Why don't you go on, Holly? I'll close up here."

"Are you sure?" Her elder sister reached for her coat.

"Absolutely. Go home with your family. It's almost closing time, and it'll just take me a moment to lock up."

As soon as the Merkins left in a cloud of familial happiness, Jona flipped the window sign to closed, straightened the shop, and dealt with the cash drawer. Fifteen minutes later, the shop was locked, and she raced along the pavement as if she were still twelve years old.

Although the house was empty when she arrived, and no dinner simmered on the stove, Jona could not have cared less. She took the stairs two at a time in a bid to reach the desk in her room more quickly. When she pounced on the Wizard Farland's letter box, she was delighted to discover a new letter awaited her. A flush of pleasure ensued, as always.

Jona plucked out Lee's latest missive, but as she sat down to read it, her waist-length hair fell forward to block her view. With a sound of exasperation, she twisted her mane into a knot and speared it with one of the feathered quills she kept in a glass on the desk. Then, she settled down to read.

My Dear Jona,

I can't believe I'll soon be turning twenty-one! Suddenly, I feel so old. Her Majesty, The Dragon, is giving yet another wretched birthday party for me. I'm certain to have a miserable time without you there to help me laugh at myself.

The Dragon is pressing me as to my plans after I graduate from university. She intends for me to go into the military, but I'm more inclined to run away and join the circus. What do you think?

Your friend,

Lee

Without delay, Jona pulled a fresh piece of stationary toward her and dipped a quill into an inkwell to write out a response.

Dearest Lee,

Twenty-one years old is absolutely ancient! Perhaps you should ask Mr. Phipps to lend you his walking stick. In all seriousness, your aunt is quite severe, but she cares for you a great deal. I'm sure she doesn't mean for the party to be a punishment, and I expect it shall be wonderful fun. As to your future plans, well, the circus sounds delightful! Perhaps I'll join the circus, too, and learn how to wrangle elephants. When you ask Mr. Phipps for the loan of his walking stick, ask his career advice. His judgment has always been trustworthy.

Yours always,

Jona

After the ink was dry, she folded her letter into quarters, tucked it into the box, and closed the lid. After a long pause, she peeked inside, to make sure the letter had vanished. Although the box never failed to work just as the Wizard Farland had designed it, she always checked. She simply couldn't get used to magic.

A somewhat battered old trunk, her gift from the queen, sat at the foot of the bed. She opened it to lay Lee's most recent missive on top. Bundles of his previous correspondence, tied neatly with slender satin ribbons, were arranged chronologically. Since the trunk was completely full of letters, she would need to buy another trunk to store the ones going forward. Over the last nine years, Lee had sent her messages about his lessons and travels. He'd written about Hanna and Mr. McKinney's wedding, and how he'd been asked to give away the bride. In turn, Jona had written Lee to tell him her sister was getting married. Later on, she'd shared the joys of becoming an aunt. To her pleasure, his enthusiasm for correspondence never seemed to flag.

With a happy sigh, Jona went downstairs to see about preparing her evening meal. Perhaps, if she were lucky, Lee would respond to her letter before bedtime.

SEVERAL DAYS LATER, a letter written on heavy stationery arrived at the Haever Tea Shop.

Holly frowned as she peered at the envelope. "It's for you, Jona—from a Mr. Phipps. I don't recognize the name."

"Mr. Phipps is Lee's tutor." Puzzled, Jona broke the wax seal on the envelope and read the letter to herself. A thrill of excitement made her gasp. "I'm going to a party at Meridian Palace!"

Holly peered at her. "It's a royal invitation?"

"Well, no, it's actually a secret invitation from Mr. Phipps. I'm to attend the party as a surprise for Lee." She giggled. "My hair and dress must be *perfect*. Who is the best dressmaker in Ramshorn Village?"

Holly gave her a look of pity. "Oh, Jona, don't go."

Jona's spine straightened. "Why would you say that? It's Lee's birthday and I wouldn't miss it for anything."

"Royals and commoners don't marry each other, that's why. It's against the law." Holly shook her head. "You're getting your hopes up for nothing."

"You think I want to marry Lee?" Jona forced a smile to her lips. "The thought never entered my mind."

"Has it not? You've been writing him almost daily for the last nine years."

"Well I—" Jona broke off, confused. "We're best friends, and best friends write to one another."

"If you're such good friends, why didn't he invite you to his birthday party himself?"

The question seemed to hang in the air.

"You know why, Holly." Jona grabbed a dust cloth and began wiping down the display case glass. "His aunt wouldn't allow it. I daresay if she knew we were corresponding, she'd forbid it."

Holly went behind the counter, to straighten the tins on the shelves. "If the prince truly cared for you, he would have sent you a personal invitation."

Jona stared at her sister, stung. "That's rather harsh. I expect Lee is thinking of my feelings rather than his own. He's probably convinced the queen would try to embarrass me if I attended the party."

"I don't want you hurt either. There are plenty of men in Ramshorn Village who would love to put a smile on your face." Holly gave Jona a sidelong glance. "Wallace Vanderbleat, for one."

"Ugh. Wallace Vanderbleat has no imagination whatsoever, and he's stuck on himself something awful."

"Wallace is a very nice man, quite good-looking, and he

fancies you. You could certainly do a lot worse than the mayor's son."

Jona stashed her dust cloth underneath the cash register. "I'm not interested in marriage!"

"Aren't you? You are wonderful to Boyd. Don't you want children of your own?"

"Maybe." Jona averted her eyes and shrugged. "Someday."

"I advise you to forget about Prince Lee and concentrate on finding someone else." Holly's tone was kind. "Otherwise, you'll never be happy."

"You've got this all wrong." Jona opened a book of orders to be delivered later that afternoon. "I'm going to the party to surprise my best friend and wish him a happy birthday. Mr. Phipps is even sending a carriage for me, like before."

"It's not like before, is it?" Holly studied her. "You're a grown woman now, and a beautiful one at that."

Jona set about filling the first delivery order on the list. "Lee doesn't care about things like that."

Holly's snort was unladylike. "I can assure you, he does."

Although Jona loved her sister, the conversation had become annoying. "Are you going to help me with the dress or not? If I don't look like I belong at the party, someone will tell Her Majesty and I'll be escorted from the palace by the guards."

"I'll help you on one condition." Holly carried over the delivery crate and set it on the counter. "After you return to Ramshorn Village, you'll go out with Wallace Vanderbleat. I think he'll improve on closer acquaintance."

Holly's gaze made Jona squirm. "I'll consider it."

"Is that the best you can do?" Her sister sniffed. "Best of luck getting a suitable dress on your own."

Jona gritted her teeth. "Yes, I'll go out with him!"

"Good. Seriously, Jona, I beg you to put any romantic notions about Prince Lee aside. Otherwise, this episode will end very badly for you." Holly pulled her into a hug.

~

Despite Holly's bleak assessment of the situation, she accompanied Jona to the dressmaker the following day and helped design a ball gown more breathtaking than Jona could have imagined. Although the little pearls and rhinestones embroidered on the ice blue satin skirt weren't genuine jewels, they were beautiful, nonetheless. After several fittings over the course of the next few weeks, Jona tried on the completed gown and admired her reflection in the mirror. As she turned, the trim caught the light and looked dazzling.

"This gown is almost magical. It reminds me of the one the Wizard Farland conjured—but this one will last for more than one waltz!"

Holly nodded her approval. "You'll be second to none at the party. I hate to say this, but you've grown prettier than I am."

Jona felt a rush of gratitude toward her sister. "That's not so, but thank you."

"After the ball, you can always use the dress as a wedding gown. We'll just add a simple comb and veil." Holly held up a length of white netting, to judge the effect.

Jona drank in her reflection. "When I was a little girl, you told me I'd want to be pretty and ladylike one day. I guess you were right."

Holly gave her an appraising glance. "I'm right about a lot of things, but I wish I weren't."

"You're not going on about nonsense again, are you?" Jona rolled her eyes. "Truly, you've nothing to worry about...except perhaps for running the shop alone while I'm away."

"Well, if you're to have a broken heart, I suppose you should get it over with sooner rather than later." Holly returned the bolt of netting to its shelf. "At least you'll have Wallace Vanderbleat around afterward, to help you mend things."

Jona tossed her head. "Never mind that. I still need to pick out some shoes and decide how to arrange my hair!"

~

Meridian Palace

ON THE DAY of Lee's birthday party, a royal carriage arrived to pick Jona up quite early in the morning. When she finally arrived at the palace several hours later, the grounds were bustling with preparations. Wagons were offloading flowers, baskets of food, musicians, and entertainers, so Jona passed through the crowd without drawing any notice at all.

Nanny Phipps whisked her upstairs, to her old room. The bedchamber seemed surprisingly small to Jona now, but the good memories remained.

"It's wonderful to see you, lass." Nanny beamed. "The prince will be so thrilled you've come. How did you manage to keep it a secret?"

"It was awful not telling him." Jona sighed. "We usually write each other almost every day...although for some reason I haven't heard from him lately."

"The lad has been busy, being fitted for a uniform. He's to wear it to the ball."

"I hadn't thought of that." Jona frowned. "Do you think Lee will recognize me?"

"It might take him a moment or two." Nanny gave her an admiring glance. "You're grown into a stunning young lady, I must say."

Jona tried to keep a wistful note from her voice. "I hope he thinks so."

A servant muscled Jona's trunk through the door and set it down against the wall. Nanny opened the lid to reveal a profusion of blue satin.

The woman gasped with pleasure as she lifted out the iridescent ball gown. "Isn't this lovely! I'll just give this a quick press, and you'll be the prettiest girl at the party tonight."

Jona winced. "Does…does Her Majesty know I'm here?"

Nanny hesitated. "What the queen doesn't know won't hurt her. If she attends Lee's birthday party at all, it will be only for a few minutes. With so many young people about, you'll blend in."

She carried the gown from the room and disappeared from view. Although Jona had gleaned little reassurance from Nanny's answer, she brushed aside any apprehension. Hugging herself with happiness, she danced around the room. She had been yearning to see Lee so much that she would have walked from Ramshorn Village on foot, if need be.

That evening, Nanny helped Jona dress and then arranged her hair in the latest style. When a knock came on the door, Jona's stomach seemingly turned a somersault. "That's not Lee, is it?"

"No. Forgive us for interfering, Jona, but Mr. Phipps and I called upon an old friend to escort you to the party."

Nanny opened the door to reveal an elderly man, elegantly attired in formal evening wear and a fingertip-length black cape.

Jona jumped to her feet in delight. "Wizard Farland!"

"The very same." As he regarded her, his blue eyes twinkled. "You've become a beauty, my dear. I rather had a notion you would." His sigh was dramatic. "If only I were sixty years younger."

Nanny chortled with laughter. "If you were sixty years younger, you'd still be too old for her!"

"Alas." Farland held out his arm. "Shall we?"

The wizard escorted Jona down the main staircase, and the excited feeling in her midsection turned to nerves. More than once, she had to remind herself not to clutch the man's elbow too tightly. Orchestral music drifted from the ballroom and reached her ears. Would she remember how to dance when the time came?

After they reached the ground floor, she and Farland moved through the wide marble-tiled hallway and joined the end of the ballroom queue. Without making her interest too obvious, Jona craned her neck and edged sideways until she spotted the prince.

Lee stood in the hallway just outside the ballroom, greeting each new arrival with a charming, shy smile and a warm welcome. Jona's breath caught in her throat at the sight of him. A boy of twelve no longer, he was now well over six feet tall, broad of shoulder...and utterly handsome. The gold braid on his uniform jacket matched the color of his hair, giving him almost a magical glow.

A shiver of some feeling Jona couldn't quite define rippled down her spine and warmed her skin. Out of the corner of her eye, she noticed Farland glance over to gauge her reaction.

He smiled. "I see you're pleased with how our young prince has grown up."

Jona managed to laugh. "Does it really show that much?"

"Your eyes are shining, my dear. Don't worry...it adds to your considerable beauty." The wizard reached over to pat her hand. "Prince Lee is a fortunate man indeed."

Just then, an exquisite blonde in a pale-yellow gown swept past to join Lee. She slid her fingers around his arm and leaned into him, possessively. A knife-like pain twisted in Jona's midsection and she flinched. *Lee hadn't said a word about having met a girl. Is that why he hasn't written to me recently?*

Suddenly, Jona knew it had been a colossal mistake for her to come.

MAGICAL MISPERCEPTION

"*P*lease, Farland—" Jona began, but it was too late. Lee had already spotted the wizard.

"Farland!" The prince gave him a broad grin and a hearty handshake. "I'm so delighted you could be here."

The wizard's smile was gracious. "Many happy returns, Your Highness."

Lee nodded toward the blonde. "I believe you already know Lady Serena?"

"Indeed." Farland bowed. "It's always a pleasure, my lady. You look exceptionally lovely this evening."

Lady Serena inclined her head in an arrogant manner which reminded Jona very much of Queen Gaia. "You're too kind."

When Lee turned his attention to Jona, a noticeable flush crept up from his collar. Despite that, no trace of recognition lit his eyes. Her heart sank even further.

"W-Will you introduce me to your g-guest, Farland?" Lee stammered.

The wizard's eyebrows rose. "Why, this is—"

Jona blurted out a response. "My name is Miss Holly, Your Highness. I'm the Wizard Farland's niece. Many happy returns."

She dipped into a curtsy. After Lady Serena flicked her the coolest of glances and briefest of smiles, Jona practically dragged an astonished Farland into the party.

Finally, when they were halfway across the room, the wizard came to a complete halt. "I refuse to budge another inch until you tell me what that was all about!"

Jona shook her head. "Lee didn't know me, Farland."

"Your appearance has changed, my dear! I barely recognized you myself, if truth be told."

"He doesn't *want* to know me. Can't you see he's with Lady Serena? I wouldn't dream of embarrassing Lee by dredging up an old and potentially embarrassing acquaintance he used to have with…well, a servant."

Farland peered at her. "You're not a servant, Jona. You're a personal friend."

"That's not how Her Majesty views me, and I can assure you Lady Serena would not approve either." Jona's throat swelled with emotion. "Really, it's better this way."

"But…oh dear. Young love is so complicated." He glanced around the room. "I believe I need a glass of champagne."

She released his arm and forced a carefree smile to her lips. "Please do enjoy yourself. It's a party after all, and there are plenty of people for me to meet."

Farland gave her a shrewd glance. "I'll return with two glasses."

He ambled off toward the champagne fountain but was waylaid by a young matron in satin and jewels. As the woman drew Farland into conversation, Jona was left alone to consider her predicament. She hadn't expected Lee to remain a bachelor forever, so why had seeing him with Lady Serena been such a blow?

Because Holly was right. I'm in love with him and didn't want to admit it.

And now here she was at the palace, a pathetic country

mouse hoping to receive crumbs from Lee's table. If there hadn't been so many people around, she would have burst into tears.

To spare Lee's feelings and salvage her own shredded dignity, Jona decided to leave the party quietly. The prince was still busy greeting his guests at the door, so that exit was unavailable to her. Nevertheless, she could easily slip onto the veranda without any difficulty at all. A casual stroll in the garden would take her out of view, and then she'd creep back to her room, unseen.

As she moved through the crowd, however, people seemed to be staring at her. Evidently, her dress was inappropriate and it was obvious she didn't belong.

A young man in evening clothes intercepted Jona and sketched a formal bow. "The dancing is about to start. May I have the first dance?"

Trapped by good manners, she had no choice but to accept. "Thank you, yes."

As the orchestra began to play, Lee started off the dancing with Lady Serena. After a short while, Jona's partner led her to the floor, and they stepped out into a waltz. To her relief, she had no trouble following his lead.

"My name is Lord Van." His glossy black hair reflected light from the chandelier overhead. "I heard a rumor that you're Farland's niece, Miss Holly?"

Farland gave Jona a surreptitious wink as he danced past with the bejeweled matron.

"Er...yes, that's right," Jona managed.

"There are at least ten chaps who wanted to be the first to dance with you, Miss Holly, but I won the coin toss."

Lord Van preened like one of the peacocks roaming the palace grounds. Was he making a joke at her expense, or was this the way aristocrats comported themselves?

She gave him a glance of reproach. "You're teasing me."

"Indeed, I'm not! Look over there, under that gas lamp nearest the orchestra." He nodded toward the corner. "We all know each other from university, and we're a competitive lot."

Her gaze slid past Lord Van and settled on a group of young men congregated next to the piano. The chaps were indeed watching her with intense interest, and Jona fought to hide her dismay. If she were to dance with each one of them, how in the world would she ever escape?

As it turned out, Lord Van proved to be correct and she was unable to extricate herself from the party gracefully. An hour passed in which Jona barely had time to catch her breath. Every so often, she would pass Lady Serena on the dance floor. The young woman seemed always to have a slightly sour expression on her lovely features, even as her many partners were obviously enraptured by her beauty. Jona had a sudden flash of recognition; Serena was the same girl who'd danced with Lee over nine years ago, at the end-of-summer ball.

I should have guessed she was intended for him, even back then.

Although Jona hadn't sat down since her arrival at the party, she noticed Lee seemed to prefer his conversation with Farland to the dance floor. Certainly, the wizard was too much of a gentleman to reveal Jona's true identity, but she worried the elderly man might let something slip by accident. She'd die a thousand deaths if she was revealed to be an imposter in front of all these elegant people—especially the superior Lady Serena!

When Lord Van came to claim Jona for yet another dance, Lee appeared at his elbow. "Forgive me, Van, but I've not yet had the pleasure of dancing with Miss Holly."

A frown passed over Lord Van's face. "Since it's your birthday, Your Highness, I suppose it would be unpardonable for me not to yield."

"You are very gracious."

Lord Van backed away, leaving Jona face-to-face with the prince at last.

"Shall we?" Lee made a gesture of invitation.

Jona knew he was asking her to dance merely out of respect for the wizard, but she couldn't think of a ready excuse to decline. Truth be told, part of her rejoiced at the opportunity to be in his arms, if only for a few minutes.

She sank into a deep curtsy, as gracefully as she knew how. "Thank you, Your Highness. It would be an honor."

Even as Lee took her hand and slid his other one around her waist, she couldn't bring herself to meet his gaze. Instead, she fixed her eyes firmly on his slightly crooked cravat, stifling the impulse to straighten it for him.

Dancing with Lee again was strangely familiar and yet entirely new. Although she desperately wanted to speak, suddenly no remark seemed witty or clever enough to engage him in conversation. When his attention was momentarily diverted by the clatter of a dropped tray, she allowed herself to admire his handsome face. She remembered the slight cleft in his chin and how his eyebrows had always arched in a mischie-vous fashion that used to make her laugh. In so many ways, he was the same Lee she'd always known...except that he was in love with another woman. The thought nearly made Jona stumble.

Lee's arm tightened around her. "Are y-y-you all right, Miss Holly?"

Shame spread through her when Jona heard Lee fighting his stutter again. To him, she was a complete stranger, so she felt entirely to blame for his uneasiness.

"I'm fine, thank you, Your Highness." She gave him an encouraging smile. "Please forgive me. I'm often a little clumsy dancing with gentlemen I haven't met before."

Lee took a deep breath. "I didn't kn-know F-Farland h-had a n-niece."

He was flushed red with embarrassment, but Jona pretended not to notice.

"Actually, I only recently discovered he was my uncle. Apparently, he and my mother never got along."

"I thought F-Farland w-was an o-only ch-child."

That came as news to Jona, but she masked her surprise. "Er...Uncle Farland thought as much for many years. My mother is his half-sister on his father's side. It's all a bit scandalous, really."

Squirming inwardly at her deceit, Jona wondered if the waltz would never end.

"Are y-you m-m-magical, too?"

Scarlet stained Lee's face, and his humiliation was Jona's own. She simply couldn't watch his suffering anymore. "Come on, Lee, you can do it! Just imagine I'm wearing trousers!"

He stopped waltzing and stared at her as if he'd seen a ghost. "What?"

"Forgive me, Your Highness," she gasped. "I shouldn't have said that."

She pulled away and hastened toward the veranda. Outside at last, Jona felt the cool night air on her burning skin as she stumbled past the chestnut tree and into the rose garden. The palace grounds were cloaked in darkness, but with tears blurring her vision she couldn't see much anyway.

She heard footsteps approaching, and Lee's voice rang out. "Jona?"

Her heart sank as she wheeled around. "I'm so sorry, Lee. I didn't mean to spoil your birthday party just now. Mr. Phipps asked me to come as a surprise, but I didn't realize..." her voice trailed off.

A muscle worked in his jaw. "You answered Mr. Phipps' invitation, but you wouldn't answer mine?"

"What are you talking about? I never received any invitation from you."

"I sent a royal invitation, Jona, by messenger. When you

didn't respond, I thought perhaps you might have met someone and didn't want to hurt my feelings."

She blinked. "Is that why you haven't written lately? No, I haven't met anyone. And I never received your invitation."

A flash of anger lit Lee's eyes. "The Dragon intercepted it." He paused a moment. "I'm glad you're here, but you should have told me who you were right off."

"With Lady Serena by your side, it was not appropriate." Jona forced a smile to her lips. "I'm very happy for you, Lee. I'm sure she'll make a lovely bride."

"For somebody else, maybe." When he snorted, she could almost see the twelve-year-old Lee again. "I don't care two figs for her, Jona. She's a snob and boring to boot."

"But…why was she standing next to you in the receiving line?"

"Serena's been conspiring with The Dragon, trying to get me to propose. I've no intention of it." He drew close enough to take her hand. "Come back to the party, Miss Jona Haever. Now that you're here, I can finally enjoy myself."

Jona hesitated. "Oh, Lee, your friends could tell I don't belong. Everybody was staring."

"They were staring because you're so beautiful! I couldn't tear my eyes away from you, either." Lee brushed a kiss onto the back of her hand, and Jona melted inside. "Please come dance with me. I rather like being the most envied man in the room."

The joy she felt at being with him once more was so intense, she wasn't entirely certain why she wasn't glowing with light. Thereafter, even with its bad beginning, she could not recall having ever had a better evening. Lee was so relaxed with her by his side he didn't stammer once the entire time. Lady Serena scowled in their direction occasionally, but Jona didn't let it bother her overmuch. Queen Gaia's appearance halfway through the party gave Jona a few rough moments, but the queen just waved at everyone and left shortly thereafter. The woman didn't even stay long enough to watch Farland's wonderful magic show.

At the end of the party, after the last guest had departed, Lee wouldn't let Jona go. "It's my birthday." His eyes were mischievous. "Surely you wouldn't deny me a little conversation."

"I would never deny you conversation, birthday or not."

He escorted her to the library, where they curled up on the window seat to talk. Finally, after the clock struck three, Jona stifled a yawn.

"This has been so wonderful, Lee, but I'd better head off to bed. Otherwise, I'm going to fall asleep and start to snore."

Lee's somewhat sleepy expression was replaced by a sudden intensity. "Before you go, I want to show you something."

He reached into his pocket and pulled out a folded red hair ribbon. Although it was old and slightly frayed, she recognized it instantly.

Jona met his gaze. "Isn't that—"

"A part of you has been with me always, ever since you left here. Now that you're back, I don't want to lose you again."

Lee took Jona in her arms and kissed her with such sweet tenderness, she knew she could never love anyone but him.

"If we were to marry, hypothetically speaking, and we couldn't live at the palace any longer, would you consider running away to the circus with me?" he murmured, in between kisses.

"Hypothetically speaking, and in all other ways, I would go anywhere with you."

They clung together until the sun began to lift the darkness over the palace grounds.

Albeit reluctantly, Lee escorted Jona to her room. "I'll see you in a few hours, my love." He kissed her a few more times for good measure. "We'll plan our escape then."

As Jona undressed and fell into bed, it felt as if the blood in her veins had been replaced by champagne.

Little did she know her ebullience would be short-lived.

DESPITE GETTING VERY LITTLE SLEEP, Jona vaulted out of bed with a smile on her face. The morning was every glorious holiday rolled up into one—with Lee as the gift. After she dressed as quickly as possible, she attempted to drag a brush through her hair. Since her tresses were still in a mass of curls from the night before, she gave up and simply tied her hair back with a ribbon. The arrangement of her hair mattered little when Lee was sure to mess it up with his fingers.

A loud knock came at her door. Jona giggled, assuming it was Lee, or perhaps Nanny, but she was wrong. A pair of guards stood in the hallway, glowering down at her with contempt in their expressions. Jona stared at them, wide-eyed and speechless.

The taller of the two rested his hand on the haft of his sword. "Miss Haever, Her Majesty requests your presence, immediately."

The statement was not a request, but a command, and not one issued in good humor. A clammy chill spread through Jona's body as she accompanied the guards downstairs.

When she passed through the doorway of the queen's breakfast room, she saw Lee sitting in a chair, flanked by two guards of his own. With a clenched jaw and his muscles drawn taut, his expression could not have been more wretched.

When he spotted Jona, Lee sprang to his feet. Before he could step toward her, however, the guards physically restrained him by the arms.

Jona burst into tears. "What's happening, Lee?"

He struggled to free himself. "Don't worry, Jona. No matter what The Dragon says, she'll never keep us apart."

"Such drama." Queen Gaia finished a piece of buttered toast in a leisurely fashion and wiped her fingers with a linen napkin.

Jona had never been more angry in her life. "Let Lee go! Can't you see the guards are hurting him?"

The older woman ignored her pleas. "Now then…a certain relationship has come to light—one that requires my intervention. Be under no illusion that this silly liaison between the two of you, such as it is, can continue. I shall very shortly be announcing the betrothal of my nephew to Lady Serena."

"Announce whatever you wish, Your Majesty. There is only one woman I will ever love or consent to wed," Lee snapped.

The queen gave him a bland smile. "You are quite mistaken." In the next moment, she fixed her icy gaze on Jona. "It was exceedingly crass of you to come to the palace without an invitation, my girl, but I expect no better from a vulgar commoner."

Lee made a sound of frustration. "I sent Jona an invitation, as you very well know!"

"Hmm." Queen Gaia rose. "You will be escorted to the palace gates at once, Miss Haever, and you will be obliged to make your way home as best you can. If you attempt to have any further contact with my nephew, or any member of my staff, you will be arrested and dealt with in the harshest possible fashion. It goes without saying that the Royal Warrant is revoked from your family's wretched tea shop. Do I make myself clear?"

Unabashed tears spilled down Jona's face. "I used to tell Lee that you had his best interests at heart. Now, I realize you're heartless."

The woman made a dismissive gesture. "Guards, remove this creature from my presence."

Lee's voice rang out. "Nobody touch her!"

He shoved the guard nearest him to the floor, and before the other one could react, he grabbed the man's sword from its scabbard. Following his lead, Jona did the same to the guards on either side of her and hastened to join Lee. With their backs against the wall, they stood together, swords at the ready, holding the men at bay.

"Captain of the Guards!" Queen Gaia cried.

With the arrival of more soldiers, Lee and Jona were completely overwhelmed. Although she was scared witless, Jona forced herself to remain calm. The situation was absolutely hopeless by any estimation, and she knew it. When she exchanged a glance with Lee, she could see from his expression, he knew it, too.

She tried unsuccessfully to keep her sword hand from shaking. "I think we can take them, Lee."

He brandished his sword. "Definitely."

A commotion could be heard in the hallway outside the breakfast room, and a deep, commanding voice rang out.

"Out of my way!"

Guards were tossed right and left as someone forced himself through their ranks. To Jona's utter shock, Mr. Phipps appeared and came to stand alongside Jona and Lee. As he did so, the tutor unsheathed the blade hidden inside his walking stick.

The queen was incredulous. "Mr. Phipps, have you lost your mind?"

"I beg you not to insert yourself into danger, Mr. Phipps!" Lee exclaimed.

"Indeed, this is not your fight, sir," Jona said. "What would Nanny say?"

Nanny's voice reverberated, from somewhere in the hallway. "She would cheer him on!"

"I cannot allow this travesty to continue." Mr. Phipps beckoned to someone in the crowd. "Farland!"

"Yes, yes." The wizard shuffled into view, less elegantly attired than usual. His hair stuck out in riotous white tufts from his head, and it was obvious from his bedroom slippers and dressing gown, he'd been roused from his bed most unwillingly.

He glanced around the room sleepily, finally taking in the drawn swords. "Oh, my. This is rather awkward, isn't it?"

"Lift the spell, Farland." Mr. Phipps' voice was filled with steely resolve. "Do it now!"

The elderly man hesitated. "Are you completely sure? Once the spell is undone, the magic cannot be reversed."

Mr. Phipps gave him a curt nod. "I command you."

"Yes, Sire." The wizard cleared his throat, muttered something under his breath, and made a motion with his hands. In the next moment, Mr. Phipps was transformed into a different man entirely—one who was much taller, very well-built, and quite good-looking for a man in his prime. In fact, he bore an uncanny resemblance to Lee.

The queen stared at the man with a shriek of astonishment. "Gaius?"

The captain of the guards, who was near Gaius in age, recognized him instantly. "Your Majesty!"

He sank to one knee and bowed his head. The other guards followed their captain's example, although some of the younger ones exchanged puzzled glances. After they sank to their knees, a woman standing in the doorway was revealed.

The queen gasped in shock. "Cara?"

Although Jona didn't recognize the woman, Nanny's plain and oversized garments hung off her lithe form. Despite her unassuming clothes, the lady was one of the handsomest women Jona had ever beheld.

Cara gave the queen a level glance. "I suppose I should thank you for allowing Lee to live in the palace, but I must say the years have not improved your disposition one jot. You're as arrogant and insufferable as ever."

"I concur." Gaius scowled at his younger sister. "You always were a bully, Gaia, even when we were children."

The king held out his hand, and Cara hastened to her husband's side.

Gaia fluttered with disbelief. "But you're both dead! I saw your bodies!"

Farland stifled a yawn. "An illusion."

A memory emerged in Jona's mind. "A misperception?"

"Exactly that. A magical misperception, to be precise." Farland crossed over to Gaia's breakfast table and helped himself to a rasher of crispy bacon. "Some of my best work, actually, if I do say so myself."

He popped the bacon into his mouth and reached for a freshly baked scone.

"After Lee was born, Gaia, I hoped our father would accept my marriage to a commoner and we could cast off the mantle of secrecy." Gaius gave Cara a glance filled with tenderness. "When he tried to dissolve our union instead, we chose to be together another way and raise Lee as his loyal tutor and devoted nanny."

"All my idea, naturally." Farland slathered his scone with strawberry preserves. "I do enjoy a good love story."

"But now our son is facing the exact same dilemma!" Cara lifted her chin. "He shouldn't have to choose between love with this wonderful girl and duty to his country."

"Cara and I won't have it." Gaius pointed at his sister. "I hereby claim my rightful place as monarch of Meridian. My first order of business will be to change this confounded, antiquated marriage law that serves no purpose whatsoever except to inflict unhappiness."

Farland reached for the tea pot. "Hear, hear."

Stunned, Lee stared at his mother and father. Cara took her son's face in her hands and burst into tears. Lee's sword clattered to the ground, and he wrapped his arms around his mother as if he would never let her go.

"Your father and I are so proud of you," Cara whispered. "We always have been."

King Gaius embraced Cara, Lee, and Jona, and only the most hard-hearted of persons in the room was unmoved. Even Gaia was sobbing, although Jona could not be entirely certain if it was due to the return of her brother or to the loss of her throne.

The End

EPILOGUE

The transition of power in Meridian was swift and remarkable only for its smoothness. The citizens of Meridian accepted the return of long-lost King Gaius with enthusiasm, since the telling of the tale made for great sport in drawing rooms, inns, and taverns across the kingdom.

In addition, when Prince Lee's engagement to commoner Jona Barbara Haever was announced, the occasion for a royal wedding was one for celebration...except by Wallace Vanderbleat, Lady Serena, and her family. Thereafter, Princess Jona was seen as a trendsetter and started a whole new fashion with trousers for women.

Former Queen Gaia went on an extended tour of Meridian, as a sort of goodwill ambassador for the monarchy. She was excellent at ribbon-cutting ceremonies, speech making, and school dedications. The dancing instructor, Mr. Rapp, accompanied her on her travels, and several eyebrows were raised when they quietly eloped.

Jona and Lee lived happily ever after—until their own children were born, that is, and began to get into every sort of mischief...particularly their daughter.

Evan put down his spoon. "All right, Miss Westerfield, let's review some history. After your father's accident, an anonymous donor set up a full scholarship for you at Aldesbury Magic Academy. Even though you were one of the most talented youngsters the school had ever tested, your father refused to let you attend. Thereafter, you've secretly been studying magic on your own."

She gasped. "How could you possibly know that?"

"I told him." Thaddeus fixed his brown eyes on Minna over the rims of his glasses. "Once your father refused his permission for you to matriculate at the Academy, your dear mother quietly contacted me to ask about booklists for homeschooled wizards."

"My mother contacted the Head Wizard of Ceresland about me?" Minna peered at him. "I'd no idea."

"Nancy believed your father was in no state of mind to forbid you from developing your abilities. Ordinarily, I would have refused to interfere, but I dislike talent going to waste. After some deliberation, I agreed to oversee your education. I kept in constant contact with her regarding your progress and even came to visit you twice a year."

"I don't mean to be difficult, but I don't recall having been introduced to you before today."

"Oh, I wasn't myself. No, I was Mr. Bodkins, the short fat jolly fellow from the fictitious Homeschooled Students for Sorcery Board of Education."

Her jaw dropped. "That was you?"

His eyes twinkled as he smoothed down his beard. "In disguise. As you see, I'm far more handsome than Mr. Bodkins."

Evan swallowed a bite of potato. "Now that your training isn't a secret any longer, Miss Westerfield, will you join us?"

"Legally, I can't. I haven't taken my wizard exam yet, and if the authorities catch me practicing wizardry without a proper license, I could be barred from the practice of magic altogether."

"Your work is permitted as long as it's under my direct supervision." Thaddeus nodded at Evan. "If it sets your mind at ease, my apprentice doesn't have his license either. He won't be sitting for the exam until it's offered this fall."

"I've registered for that particular exam as well." She bit her lower lip. "I just have to find the right moment to break it to my father."

Evan blinked. "You're over eighteen, Minna. Your father has to let you go sometime."

"You make it sound simple, but you don't know him like I do." She sighed. "I-I have a few days before he gets back from his business trip. Could we get the rift sealed before then?"

"Possibly so, but it won't be easy." Thaddeus counted off the challenges on his fingers. "We must first travel to the parallel dimension, locate the wizard responsible for creating the rift, and then bring him back to face justice. He used a purloined magical letter opener to breach the barrier, and we can't fail to retrieve it."

"And we have to do all that without a fuss," Evan said. "You see, the letter opener is Mr. Bartholomew's."

Her eyebrows rose. "Oh?"

"The thief broke into my house and stole it." Thaddeus scowled. "If anyone else discovers such an object exists, chaos would be unleashed."

The corners of her lips quirked up in a smile. "I suppose having unlicensed wizards on the case would help keep the matter under wraps."

"Yes, but there's also the question of motivation." Thaddeus's gaze slid toward his apprentice. "My apprentice believes you're perfect for the task."

She gave Evan a quizzical glance. "I can't imagine why."

Evan cleared his throat. "The thief is Ned Rooney. I thought perhaps you might enjoy the task of catching him."

Her smile faded and she grew pale. "I see."

ABOUT THE AUTHOR

Author Suzanne G. Rogers is a California native, but she changed coastlines and now lives in romantic Savannah, Georgia, on an island populated by deer, exotic birds, turtles, otters, and gators.

ALSO BY SUZANNE G. ROGERS

FANTASY

<u>Standalone Titles</u>

Clash of Wills

Dani & the Immortals

*The Dragon Rider's Daughter**

Magical Misperception

Tournament of Chance: Dragon Rebel

*Whimsical Tendencies**

Something Wicked in L.A.

Royal Promenade

<u>The Yden Series</u>

The Last Great Wizard of Yden (Book One)

Dragon Clan of Yden (Book Two)

Secrets of Yden (Book Three)

Kira (Prequel to the Yden Trilogy)

*Available in audiobook format

ALSO BY SUZANNE G. ROGERS
HISTORICAL ROMANCE

The Mannequin Series

*The Mannequin** (Book One)

Grace Unmasked (Book Two)

The Star-Crossed Seamstress (Book Three)

A Chance of Rayne (Book Four)

The Substitute (Book Five)

The Gilded Age Series

Duke of a Gilded Age (Book One)

Lady of a Gilded Age (Book Two)

The Beaucroft Girls Series

Ruse & Romance (Book One)*

Rake & Romance (Book Two)*

Graceling Hall Series

Larken (Book One)*

Lord Apollo & the Colleen (Book Two)

The Vanishing Beauty (Book Three)

An Unexpected Romance (Book Four)

Standalone Titles

A Gift for Fiona

*My Fair Guardian**

Lady Fallows' Secrets

*Spinster**

*Jessamine's Folly**

*The Ice Captain's Daughter**

Rumer Has It

An American in Paris of the West

The Glass Heart

The Prettier Sister

One Little Kiss

Courtship on Eaton Square

**Available in audiobook format*

www.ingramcontent.com/pod-product-compliance
Lightning Source LLC
Chambersburg PA
CBHW061352140726
47997CB00003B/1171